THE
KOREAN WAR

BY TOM STREISSGUTH

Published by The Child's World®
1980 Lookout Drive • Mankato, MN 56003-1705
800-599-READ • www.childsworld.com

ACKNOWLEDGMENTS
The Child's World®: Mary Berendes, Publishing Director
Red Line Editorial: Editorial direction
The Design Lab: Design
Amnet: Production
Content Consultant: George Kallander, Associate Professor of
History, Syracuse University

Photographs ©: TSgt John C. Slockbower, cover; The Design
Lab, 5; US Army, 7; Max Desfor/AP Images, 8; AP Images,
10, 20; Charles Gorry/AP Images, 11; Department of Defense,
15; Sgt Frank C. Kerr, USMC, 17, 18; Jim Pringle/AP Images,
13, 23; George Sweers/AP Images, 27

Design Element: Shutterstock Images

ISBN 9781631437106
LCCN 2014945399

Printed in the United States of America
Mankato, MN
January, 2015
PA02259

ABOUT THE AUTHOR

Tom Streissguth was born in Washington, D.C., and grew up in Minnesota. He has worked as a teacher, book editor, and freelance author and has written more than 100 books of nonfiction for young readers. In 2014 he founded The Archive, a publishing company that compiles the nonfiction works and journalism of renowned American authors.

TABLE OF
CONTENTS

CHAPTER ONE

THE WAR BEGINS

★ ★ ★

The Chosin Reservoir lies among the steep hills of northern Korea. There are few roads or settlements in the area. In the fall of 1950, U.S. Marine and Army units reached the banks of the reservoir. They were close to the North Korean border with China.

Narrow roads made it tough to move across the countryside. Icy winds blew through the hills. The frozen ground prevented troops from building barriers or **foxholes**. But the armies of the United States, South Korea, and other **United Nations (UN)** countries were on the move. The North Korean troops were retreating. The war had lasted only a few months. Now it seemed to be almost over.

The Korean War had begun in the summer of 1950. The North Korean army had invaded South Korea. The United States was now landing troops and pushing the North Koreans back.

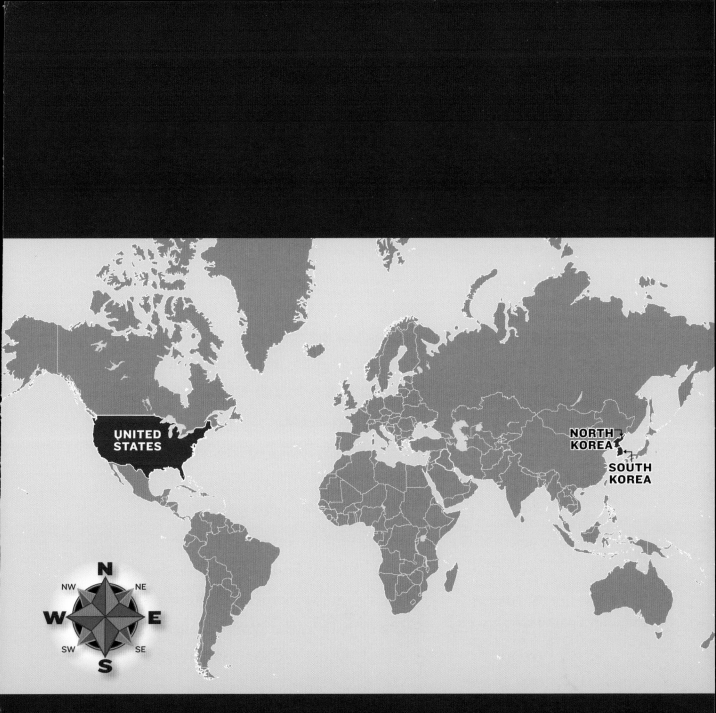

UNITED STATES

NORTH KOREA

SOUTH KOREA

N
NW   NE
W   E
SW   SE
S

In October, the United States prepared to invade North Korea and end the war. But on October 25, North Korea's ally, China, entered the war. At Chosin, the Chinese attacked in waves. Many Chinese troops died from **mortars** and machine gun fire from the U.S. troops. But thousands more Chinese soldiers came over the hills. Their terrifying assaults overran the U.S. Marine positions.

SIGNAL PANELS

Wartime can cause confusion between troops. Military troops attach signal panels to their trucks during wartime. The colors change daily. Planes can quickly identify which trucks belong to the enemy, or they can drop supplies to their own troops. During the Korean War, there was confusion about the color of the signal panels on the trucks. One time, U.S. Air Force Lt. Col. Bud Biteman could not identify a group of ten military vehicles. Biteman's plane was armed with bombs, rockets, and machine guns. He was supposed to attack, but he held his fire. Later he learned there were no friendly troops in the area. The trucks he spotted belonged to the North Korean army.

RETREAT TO THE 38TH PARALLEL

After 17 days of battle, some U.S. Marine units regrouped. They moved away from Chosin Reservoir by retreating 100 miles (160 km). The U.S. Marines fought the Chinese troops along narrow dirt roads to the North Korean coast. Ships rescued thousands of troops and civilians from the port of Hungnam. Other troops reached the **demilitarized zone** that divided Korea in half. This

U.S. troops near the 38th parallel wait for the signal to fire against the enemy.

line is called the 38th parallel because it lies near 38 degrees latitude north. The soldiers built positions here during the winter. They dug deep into the hard ground. Tents were raised and they set up heavy guns. Night patrols watched for enemy soldiers.

U.S. troops crouch in the bushes along the 38th parallel. They are on the lookout for North Korean troops.

The Korean War turned into a **stalemate**. Neither side could advance into enemy territory. There were many short fights but few major battles. Over three years, more than 30,000 U.S. troops died. Many Korean civilians also died from the fighting.

Both North Korea and the United States took thousands of prisoners. Many prisoners died from hunger and from harsh treatment. Some disappeared, but others returned home. At the end of the war, Korea remained divided between North and South.

ANOTHER VIEW

There were many different armies fighting in Korea. The United States was part of a large coalition. U.S. soldiers fought alongside troops from Great Britain, South Korea, Canada, and Australia. Turkey, Thailand, and the Philippines also sent troops to fight. All of these nations agreed to fight under the flag of the United Nations. The United States had the largest military force, but it worked with foreign commanders and troops. Imagine you were a U.S. military leader. You must work with other countries' leaders and you may not always agree. Do you believe fighting as part of a coalition makes it easier or harder to win a war?

CHAPTER TWO

THE INVASION OF SOUTH KOREA

★ ★ ★

Kim Il Sung

The empire of Japan absorbed Korea in 1910. Japan surrendered to the United States at the end of World War II (1939–1945). When the Japanese left Korea, the U.S. and Soviet Union armies arrived. The United States occupied southern Korea, and troops of the Soviet Union remained in the north. The 38th parallel divided the two sides.

A DIVIDED COUNTRY

The United States and the Soviet Union agreed Korea should hold elections to choose new leaders. The Soviet

Syngman Rhee, *right*, and U.S. Gen. Douglas MacArthur sit together at a ceremony in Seoul.

Union supported Kim Il Sung as the ruler of North Korea.
The United States supported Syngman Rhee as president of
South Korea in 1948.

The new leaders wanted to reunite Korea, but they could not agree on the best form of government. The **Communist** party led North Korea. The government controlled all property and industry. South Korea allowed its citizens to own property. But in the late 1940s, many South Koreans saw their democratic government as corrupt. There were protests and violent rebellions. The police and the army harshly put down these uprisings. Many South Koreans living in the countryside died or fled their homes. Others lost their land and property.

With a weakened South Korean government, the United States feared Communism would spread to South Korea. U.S. military advisers helped the South Korean government keep tight control over its people and territory.

Many civilians and soldiers suffered from illnesses during the Korean War. Troops lived in dirty camps. Germs spread through water and food. An **epidemic** of **smallpox** broke out in North Korea. Thousands of civilians caught the deadly disease. The Chinese accused the United States of using germ warfare, or intentionally using bacteria to harm or kill the North Koreans.

ALONG THE 38TH PARALLEL

North and South Korea had troops stationed along the 38th parallel. There were frequent battles across the line. There was

South Korean troops make their way to the 38th Parallel to fight the North Korean troops.

GERM WARFARE

Chinese newspapers ran stories about U.S. planes dropping infected insects over Korea during the Korean War. They claimed the United States was making civilians and soldiers sick on purpose. The United States denied this. Chinese newspapers stopped running the stories at the end of the war. Many North Koreans still believe they were the targets of germ warfare during the war.

heavy gun fighting at times in the border region. Troops on both sides were killed in firefights.

The United States and the Soviet Union withdrew their troops from South Korea in 1949. The North Korean government saw this as a chance to defeat South Korea. North Korea wanted to invade in order to reunify the country. The North Korean army was much bigger than South Korea's army. On June 25, 1950, North Korea's army invaded the South. They captured the South Korean capital city of Seoul. The Korean War had begun.

ANOTHER VIEW

President Harry Truman ordered U.S. troops to defend South Korea in 1950. Soon after, the United States announced a war against North Korea. The Korean War was unpopular in the United States. World War II had ended just five years earlier, and the public did not support another big war effort. The United States had lost troops in Europe and Asia, and thousands of soldiers returned home wounded after World War II. Many Americans did not want the United States involved in another distant conflict. They believed it was not the business of the United States. When, if ever, do you think it is okay for one country to declare war on another?

CHAPTER THREE

ON THE MARCH

★ ★ ★

A s North Korean troops stormed through South Korea, the United States sent the army's 24th Infantry Division from Japan to South Korea. Their instructions were to delay the North Korean advance. For several weeks, this was the only U.S. military unit in Korea. It had old equipment left over from World War II. The U.S. troops had few machine guns or tanks. They were not well prepared.

In August 1950, the North Koreans reached the borders of Pusan. This harbor lay in the southern region of the Korean Peninsula. The South Korean army controlled a small area around Pusan. Scattered U.S. and UN forces also defended the Pusan area.

U.S., South Korean, and British troops found themselves surrounded by the enemy. They rushed to hold off attacking

U.S. troops board a train heading north as they prepare to battle the North Korean army. ▶

A U.S. soldier burns a North Korean army camp as U.S. troops capture Inchon.

North Korean units. More troops would be arriving soon at the port of Pusan.

FIGHTING AT PUSAN

The North Koreans assaulted Pusan with large amounts of troops, but they could not get through to the harbor city. U.S. bombers took to the skies. They bombed North Korean positions from morning until night. They also damaged supply lines leading to Pusan from North Korea. Thousands of North Korean soldiers were killed in the fight.

Gen. Douglas MacArthur took command of U.S. forces in Korea. MacArthur sent a large force of marines to capture Inchon. This port lay on the west coast of South Korea near the capital city of Seoul. Inchon was behind enemy lines, but close to the 38th parallel.

The landing at Inchon was risky. U.S. troops could only get new supplies by boat, not by land. The sea currents in the port were dangerous. If a storm came up, high waves might swamp and sink the landing craft. It was the annual **monsoon** season in Korea. At this time of year, heavy storms often hit Inchon.

RETURN TO THE 38TH PARALLEL

General MacArthur gave the order to go forward. The plan was to capture Inchon and then advance to

MOBILE ARMY SURGICAL HOSPITALS

Many battles in Korea took place in areas far from cities and people. The countryside had few roads. It was hard to reach by helicopter. Wounded troops had to make a long trip to the coast to reach a hospital. Mobile Army Surgical Hospitals (MASH) set up bases in the mountains of Korea. Doctors and nurses worked close to the battlefields. They were able to quickly move when needed. The MASH units boosted the spirits of troops. They knew medics were a few miles away. This gave them a better chance to survive a serious combat injury.

The city of Inchon burned after U.S. planes dropped several bombs.

Seoul. This would cut off supply lines to North Korean troops. They would be forced back to the 38th parallel.

For several days, U.S. planes bombed Inchon. U.S. spies working in the city reported on North Korean defenses. The United States made small supply drops elsewhere in South Korea.

On September 15, U.S. Navy ships attacked Inchon from the sea. The shelling destroyed guns and barriers. Hundreds of civilians in the port died. Several hours later, U.S. forces landed. Thousands of North Korean troops fled their positions in Inchon.

U.S. and South Korean troops fought their way into Seoul. Tanks blew up enemy positions in the streets. Many North Korean soldiers surrendered. The North Korean army left Seoul within three days. They quickly retreated to the 38th parallel.

AN**O**T**H**E**R** **V**I**E**W**

Korea remains divided today. The Communist regime in North Korea has built nuclear weapons and has one of the largest armies in the world. North Korea often threatens to invade and conquer South Korea. An agreement between South Korea and the United States allows the United States to station troops, planes, guns, and other military equipment in South Korea. But some South Koreans oppose the presence of the U.S. military in their country. They believe there will be less chance of another war with North Korea if the United States leaves. Fights sometimes break out between U.S. troops and South Koreans. South Korean laws do not apply to the U.S. military. Many South Koreans believe U.S. troops should follow South Korean laws and courts. The United States still wants to prevent another invasion by North Korea. Should U.S. forces remain in South Korea?

CHAPTER FOUR

STALEMATE

★ ★ ★

The Inchon landing pushed the North Korean army back. The army eventually retreated from the 38th parallel, too. This allowed U.S. troops to advance into North Korea. They captured the capital city of Pyongyang. U.S. forces advanced close to the Yalu River. This waterway separated North Korea from China. China worried about its country's national safety. China did not want North Korea to be defeated. North Korea was an important ally. Chinese forces crossed the border. The counterattack pushed back U.S. troops.

U.S. President Harry Truman had to make a decision. The United States could try to conquer North Korea and reunite Korea, but if the war with China spread, the Soviet Union might enter the conflict. That could mean a very dangerous nuclear war in Asia.

U.S. troops and tanks make their way to the captured city of Pyongyang. ▶

GOING NUCLEAR

The Korean War posed a danger to all of East Asia. Both the United States and the Soviet Union had nuclear weapons. U.S. commanders planned to drop atomic bombs on China, but China was an ally of the Soviet Union. A nuclear attack by the United States could bring the Soviet Union into the Korean War. The Soviets could use nuclear weapons of their own. President Truman and later President Eisenhower had the nuclear option available. Many U.S. commanders believed nuclear weapons could win the war. Both Truman and Eisenhower decided against this option.

TRUMAN AND MACARTHUR

General MacArthur wanted to continue the attack and conquer North Korea. But President Truman decided against the attack. The disagreement prompted Truman to fire MacArthur.

The war remained at a standstill for two years. U.S. troops fought many short battles along the 38th parallel.

The conditions for the troops on both sides were difficult. The bombing and fighting destroyed many Korean villages and farms. There was little food available. Millions of civilians died of illness, starvation, and gunfire. Korea's bitterly cold winters took their toll on the troops stationed in the mountains.

Both sides also took many thousands of prisoners. The treatment of prisoners blocked a peace agreement. The two sides could not agree on sending prisoners home. But they agreed to Operation Little Switch in April 1953. This allowed sick and injured prisoners from both sides to return to their home countries.

ANOTHER VIEW

The North Korean army crushed U.S. forces defending South Korea in July 1950. U.S. troops were not prepared for battle. Many civilians were also caught in the crossfire. U.S. troops often could not tell an enemy soldier from a civilian. On July 25, at No Gun Ri the fighting was intense. Near the battle, several hundred civilians were fleeing the danger across a stone bridge. U.S. army troops thought they were enemy troops. The Americans opened fire with rifles and machine guns. Warplanes shot from the air. Hundreds of Korean civilians died. How can an army prevent civilian deaths in a battle zone?

CHAPTER FIVE

TRUCE

★ ★ ★

U.S. commanders believed dropping bombs from planes might break the stalemate between North Korea and South Korea. They began Operation Strangle in May 1951. The bombing destroyed roads and bridges near the 38th parallel. North Korea fought back with powerful anti-aircraft guns. These weapons threw shells high into the air. Clouds of metal pieces exploded in the path of the planes. This damaged many planes. Many bombers crashed, and crewmembers died.

FIGHTING ON THE GROUND

On the ground, Chinese and North Korean troops were able to quickly repair the damage to roads and bridges. They worked at night and undercover. The United States hoped the bombing would force China to ask for a truce. Instead, China stepped up its efforts to win the war.

Troops from both sides used trenches throughout the war. ▶

U.S. officers ordered attacks and raids on North Korean positions, but the Chinese and North Koreans were skilled at building defenses. They raised barriers and dug trenches. They also used artillery to protect their forward positions.

GUARDING THE 38TH PARALLEL

North and South Korea are still separated close to the original 38th parallel. This demilitarized zone is 2.5 miles (4 km) wide. Anyone entering the zone can be killed. The U.S. and South Korean armies send out constant patrols. North Korea has stationed guns, tanks, and thousands of troops in the area. The sides called a truce in 1953, but the Korean War never officially ended. North Korea and South Korea never signed a peace agreement. The United States promised to protect the South from another invasion from the North. It is possible that fighting could break out again.

By the end of 1951, the Korean War reached a stalemate. Neither side was strong enough to try another invasion, by land or by sea. The strong defenses made it difficult to move forward or overrun enemy positions.

A NEW PRESIDENT

In November 1952, President Dwight Eisenhower won the U.S. presidential election. He was determined to reach a peace agreement in Korea. North Korea, China, and the United States finally called a truce in July 1953.

The United States pledged to protect South Korea from North Korea. It stationed thousands of troops along the 38th parallel and throughout the country. U.S. troops still patrol this zone and watch carefully for enemy troop movements. South Korea's capital, Seoul, is only 30 miles (48 km) from the 38th parallel and the North Korean army.

ANOTHER VIEW

After the Korean War, the United States sent military advisers to Vietnam. The goal was to prevent a Communist takeover of South Vietnam by North Vietnam. American military involvement in the Vietnam War lasted more than ten years, from 1961 to 1973. North Vietnam won that war. Television news programs carried video of fighting in the Vietnam War. Reporters in the Korean War could not get near the fighting. The Korean War was the last war to take place before television became common. Many Americans were against the Korean War. However, there were few public protests against that war. During Vietnam, war protests were much larger and more common. The Vietnam War became very unpopular in the United States. It is widely believed that television news coverage of the Vietnam War increased protests against it. What role do you think television plays in conflicts around the world today?

TIMELINE

1945	World War II ends with Japan surrendering, and the Japanese army leaving Korea.
June 25, 1950	North Korea invades South Korea. The United States sends troops to stop the invasion.
September 1950	Gen. Douglas MacArthur leads the Inchon landings, pushing back North Korean troops.
1951	The Chinese army battles U.S. troops in North Korea.
March 1951	Seoul falls to North Korea but is recaptured by U.S. and South Korean armies.
July 1951	Peace talks begin.
1952	The Korean War reaches a stalemate near the 38th parallel.
July 1953	The United Nations, United States, China, and North Korea sign a truce ending the Korean War.
2014	The demilitarized zone remains between North Korea and South Korea.

GLOSSARY

coalition (koh-uh-LISH-uhn) A coalition is a group of countries that join together for a common goal. A large coalition helped fight the Korean War.

Communist (KOM-yuh-nist) A Communist government owns land, oil, factories, and ships, and there is no privately owned property. A Communist government runs North Korea.

demilitarized zone (de-MIL-uh-tur-ized ZOHN) A demilitarized zone is an area where military units are not supposed to enter or cross. The demilitarized zone runs close to the 38th parallel.

epidemic (ep-uh-DEM-ik) An epidemic is an occurrence in which a disease spreads quickly and affects many people. An epidemic of smallpox broke out in North Korea.

foxholes (FOKS-hohls) Foxholes are holes dug for soldiers to sit or lie in for protection. The ground in Korea was frozen so soldiers could not dig foxholes.

monsoon (mon-SOON) A season of heavy rain in Southeast Asia. Monsoon season happened during the Korean War.

mortars (MOR-turs) Mortars are small weapons that hurl shells short distances. Many Chinese troops died from mortars.

nuclear (NOO-klee-ur) Nuclear is a weapon that involves a nuclear reaction. The United States was afraid of nuclear weapons being used during the Korean War.

smallpox (SMAWL-poks) Smallpox is a disease that leaves permanent scars on victims and is usually fatal. An epidemic of smallpox broke out in North Korea.

stalemate (STAYL-mayt) A stalemate is a situation in which neither side can gain a victory. The Korean War came to a stalemate.

United Nations (UN) (yoo-NITED NAY-shuhns) The United Nations (UN) is a political organization established in 1945. Countries in the United Nations helped fight the Korean War.

TO LEARN MORE

BOOKS

Edwards, Paul M. *The A to Z of the Korean War.* Lanham, MD: Scarecrow Press, 2005.

Wainstock, Dennis. *Truman, MacArthur and the Korean War.* New York: Enigma Books, 2011.

WEB SITES

Visit our Web site for links about the Korean War: **childsworld.com/links**

Note to Parents, Teachers, and Librarians: We routinely verify our Web links to make sure they are safe and active sites. So encourage your readers to check them out!

INDEX